ROT

The Bravest in the World!

BEN CLANTON

atheneum

Atheneum Books for Young Readers
New York   London   Toronto   Sydney   New Delhi

For Gwen!
The Bravest in the World!

And with special thanks to my big sister,
aka Mean Green Samantha Jean, for the inspiration!

𝒜
atheneum

ATHENEUM BOOKS FOR YOUNG READERS
An imprint of Simon & Schuster Children's Publishing Division
1230 Avenue of the Americas, New York, New York 10020 · Copyright © 2020 by Ben Clanton
Photographs of medieval Viking helmet by mrdoomits/iStock; sword by MikeyGen73/iStock; bay stallion rearing by Abramova_Kseniya/iStock;
clear sky landscape by kokoroyuki/iStock; potato by belterz/iStock; and checkered tablecloth by jirkaejc/iStock
ATHENEUM BOOKS FOR YOUNG READERS is a registered trademark of Simon & Schuster, Inc.
Atheneum logo is a trademark of Simon & Schuster, Inc. · For information about special discounts for bulk purchases,
please contact Simon & Schuster Special Sales at 1-866-506-1949 or business@simonandschuster.com.
The Simon & Schuster Speakers Bureau can bring authors to your live event. For more information or to book an event,
contact the Simon & Schuster Speakers Bureau at 1-866-248-3049 or visit our website at www.simonspeakers.com.
Book design by Lucy Ruth Cummins · The text for this book was set in Typewrither.
The illustrations for this book were made using watercolors, colored pencils, potato stamps, and digital collage.
Manufactured in China · 0220 SCP · First Edition
2 4 6 8 10 9 7 5 3 1
Library of Congress Cataloging-in-Publication Data
Names: Clanton, Ben, 1988– author, illustrator.
Title: Rot, the bravest in the world! / by Ben Clanton.
Description: First edition. | New York : Atheneum Books for Young Readers, [2020] | Audience: Ages 4–8. | Audience: Grades K–1. |
Summary: Rot the mutant potato must find a way to face his fear after his big brother, Snot, tells him there may be a dangerous Squirm in the magnificent mud pit he found.
Identifiers: LCCN 2019031852 | ISBN 9781481467643 (hardcover) | ISBN 9781481467650 (eBook)
Subjects: CYAC: Fear—Fiction. | Brothers—Fiction. | Mud—Fiction. | Potatoes—Fiction. | Humorous stories.
Classification: LCC PZ7.C52923 Roq 2020 | DDC [E]—dc23
LC record available at https://lccn.loc.gov/2019031852

These are mutant potatoes.
They love mud.

They play games in it.

They eat it.

They even sleep in it.

ACK!

This is Rot.
Rot *especially* loves mud.
It is one of his favorite
things in the world.

So when Rot sees the most

magnificent, MASSIVE,

and messy mud pit EVER,

he can't wait to plunge in.

hee
hee
hee

But before he can . . .

Rot's big brother,
Snot, shouts:

Rot thinks the Squirm sounds super scary.
If only he were braver. Like a . . .

Um . . . not enough.
Rot is still one petrified potato.

But maybe if he were a . . .

Better?
Better!

But something MORE is still needed.
Something that isn't afraid to get dirty.
Something BIG! Something special.
Something like . . .

Rot takes a look in the mirror.
He *does* look ridiculous . . .

Ridiculously **AWESOME!** And **BRAVE!**

He looks like . . .

the Bravest in the World!

Rot marches up to the mud.
He puts his brave face on.
He's going in!

But wait!

Something is moving in the muck.

It's . . . it's . . .

Snot thought he had made it up too.